Thirst Of The Sea

By
Scarlet Hunter

Thirst of the Sea by Scarlet Hunter
Lucky Cl✦ver™ Publishing
Cordova, TN 38016
(The clover emblem/logo and the
seal containing name Lucky Clover is a
trademark of Lucky Cl✦ver™
Publishing)
Second Edition Copyright© 2014
ISBN: 978-0-9884676-6-8

Lucky Cl ✦ ver™ Publishing

Cover artist/illustration: VR
Editor: Leanore Elliott

Lucky Cl✤ver™ Publishing

Warning: **This book may contain graphic sexual material and/or profanity and is not meant to be read by any person under the age of 18.**

PROLOGUE

Sea of Marmara

"Why are you doing this to me?" Aretha yelled up at the star infested sky. Directing her attention at the gods, she certainly didn't see this coming. First, her morning dealt with trying to avoid being killed by human hunters and now *this*. A forced sigh pushed from her lungs as she paced in a small circle. Engulfed by a forest of trees, leaves and twigs crunched and snapped with each step her bare feet made within her sanctuary. Stopping, she ran her fingers nervously through her silvery long hair. She never imagined today would have ended up the way it did. *How did it come to this?* How could she have barely escaped hunters and then come into contact with the likes of *him* all in one day?

Him. Aretha froze thinking of the male. Her heart fluttered. His manner toward her didn't make sense. Almost as if he tried to— yes—he tried to save her from himself, but why? She'd never come across his kind before, only heard stories about those who required the blood of others to survive. Returning her glare to the night's sky, she pictured the tortured look on the man's face when he screamed for her to run. His actions were entirely contrary to the stories told about vampires, surely this was evidence he didn't wish her harm. Damn it, a pinch of nerve had her wishing she would've stayed and tried to ease his suffering. But Aretha had never encountered one of the damned before, so she didn't know how to react at first.

Kicking a small branch across the woodlot, the twinge in her arm forced her to look at the still bleeding wound making her realize the distance she put between them must have helped him. His harrowing plea for her to run came only due to him fighting his inner cravings for the substance lingering from her arm…His temptation.

Suddenly, a glow, first dim, grew brighter, illuminating the woods around her as the full moon drifted out from behind an array of clouds. Aretha glanced at the moon and laughed, perceiving the gods most likely used it like a flashlight in order to keep track of her every move. The planet earth contained a lot of darkness and evil, and not just once the sun drifted behind the sea. Aretha welcomed the moon's waves of protection while it lasted. It gave her comfort, keeping her from the dark. Sent by the gods or not, its glimmering rays always made her feel safe.

After spotting a soft patch of green moss under a tall oak tree, Aretha sat in between two roots. Its thick ancestral lines curled and wound their way reaching for earth and water to quench its thirst. Drawing her knees toward her chest, she wrapped her arms around them tightly and leaned back against the tree allowing her head to ease backwards. Tired, she lowered her heavy eyelids. Again, the vampire's face appeared in her mind. Clear, as if he stood before her now—tall, dark and full of mystery. The last intense image of the pain in his eyes as he flashed his daunting fangs burned in her brain.

Earlier, when they first encountered one another, the way his eyes followed her every move made her body tremble with fear and then excitement. Foolishly overlooking the warning of what he was, she couldn't help but wonder how those plump thick lips of his would taste. To feel the strength of his muscled arms wrap around her while her hands slid against his hardened naked chest, venturing down and across his rippled abdomen.

Aretha's eyes popped wide open stopping the delusions of what could never be. Pulling her knees in tighter, she lowered her face, resting her forehead atop her knees and emitted a heart-shattering sob. *He can never be mine, nor I his…even one of the damned. No one can. Not while this curse reigns over me.* Then to make matters worse, a burst of thunder erupted around her, followed by a downpour of rain.

Oh, for the love of…

CHAPTER ONE

"Fucking Hell!" Alaois cursed loudly at the sound of voices waking him from a rock-hard sleep. Gruffly sitting up, he willed on candles placed within numerous chiseled holes set in the four stonewalls surrounding him. The room's muggy and damp humidity from the passing night's rainstorm made him wipe perspiration from his brow. He forked his fingers through his hair before irritably rubbing the palms of his hands over his face. At the same time, he inhaled a deep breath and cursed again. Expelling air from his lungs, he growled at the voices of his brethren echoing from down the cavern hallway; the root of his interrupted rest.

Can't I get any fucking sleep around here?

Alaois flung the sheets off his naked body and grunted as he treaded toward an open closet. Still mumbling curse words, he jerked on a pair of jeans one foot at a time, before stomping into a pair of black combat boots. Heading for the door, he pulled a black muscle shirt over his broad shoulders. His palm pushed against the door's cold metal, producing an irritatingly loud squeak. He made a mental note to have one of the men slap some WD-40 on the hinges.

When he trudged down the narrow passageway, lit only by a few candles alongside the stone walls, the soles of his heavy boots splattered water out from under each step while he tucked the bottom of his shirt into the waistline of his black denim jeans. The rains this time of year always found their way inside the cracks of the walls like cockroaches to food. Yet, he preferred it that way. The wetness and moisture was perfect, keeping the coolness in the cavern at a comfortable sixty or so degrees.

After taking refuge in the cavern, hidden so deep below sea level, there would be no means to run electricity to their home. With abilities of keen sight in darkness and eyes particularly sensitive to the brightness of light, they didn't require it. Alaois and his men embraced such living. It allowed the men to escape the world of their past lives. A time of yore, in which they did everything in their power to forget atrocities committed while under blood lust and evil power.

Alaois made his way into the largest room in the cavern, their meeting spot and heart of their home while he grew more irritated. The space veered off into several tunnels that encircled around it, all leading to each of his brethren's chambers. Looking at them now, Alaois' men were gathered and they looked pissed. He knew from just one glance at each of them, having witnessed this many times, seeing their eyes dilated from their colors of blue, brown or green to a bottomless crimson red of fury. An expression meaning one of two things, hunger or a show of aggression.

Leaning his massive frame against the limestone entryway, he crossed his arms over his chest and stared while listening. Alaois scanned around the musty blood-wine stenched room at his men.

Addison, Driscoll, Braden, Dagda, and Stavros. Driscoll, only a few inches shorter than Alaois at six-five, was a sight to behold. With dirty-blond hair hanging loosely at the edges of his finely chiseled jaw-line, one couldn't help but notice the long thin scar running down the left side of his neck. A souvenir from his past, always reminding him of the creature he used to be. The very reason a mirror would never be found anywhere in Driscoll's personal chambers.

"I say we go get whoever the fuck is out there!" Driscoll insisted with his back leaning against one of the stone walls.

Alaois debated on bursting his comrade's bubble and reminding him daylight still burned on the other side. This came as no surprise to him, Driscoll never being one for assessing the obvious. But Alaois' attention turned toward Addison and Stavros.

Their elbows rested on a rectangular wooden table centered in the room, locked in an arm wrestling match. "If you do…bring it down here. I haven't had the pleasure of torturing anything in a while," Addison sneered.

The small window of distraction allowed Stavros to take full advantage of Addison and he slammed his arm down on the table. "See what happens when you take your mind off the task at hand."

Addison cracked a grin. "Best two out of three?" He wiggled his eye-brows.

Stavros huffed, released his grip on Addison's hand and removed himself from the table.

Alaois grinned and switched his gaze to the other two men, Dagda and Braden.

Their expressions revealed they were seconds away from blurting out their opinions on the subject.

All this went on while none of them sensed his presence. Alaois knew their conversations would cease the moment he made a sound, as each of them had bound themselves to following his orders and his alone. Now, Alaois stood, amused at their smack talk.

"What exactly would you do to it, Driscoll?" Braden laughed. "If you're lucky enough to catch it before we do?"

"Yeah. And you planning on going out there before briefing Alaois, or let it be another surprise? You know how well the last one went off," Dagda joked.

Finally, having had enough of their child's play, Alaois cleared his throat and entered the room. "I have a question…" He diverted his glare anywhere but at his men as he made his way into the center of the room.

All the men remained frozen in their places.

"It seems to me your heads are so far up your own asses…I guess it wouldn't make any difference if I told you the moment you took one step outside these walls, you sorry sack of shit bastards would be nothing but ash from the aftermath of the sizzling light of day. I mean, fuck…" He erupted into a flare of laughter while making his way around the room. "Since you all are so hell-bent about whatever it is on the other side, I say *go*. Don't let me fucking stop you!"

Silence lingered in the room, as Alaois directed his glare at each one of his troop of vampires. Sliding the tips of his fingers along the edge of the table's ten foot length, the only sound came from his black boots ricocheting against the rock floor and walls with each step he took. "Aww. So, I finally have your attention and yet you have nothing to say." He slammed the top of the table with his hands.

Addison leaned back in his chair as the table bucked off the ground from Alaois' forceful strike.

"Am I never to get any fucking rest around here?" The sharpness of his growl, combined with the violent boom of his fist, rattled candle sconces hanging on the walls around them.

At once, the men dropped onto one knee. Their heads slanted downward facing the ground beneath them. "My lord." They pledged in unison.

Shaking his head, temper at its breaking point, Alaois made his way over to his chair and sat at the head of the table. His head tilted to the left, then right, cracking affects from his lack of sleep echoed throughout the room. He stared fiercely at the men still kneeling before him.

Not one would dare lift their head until granted permission, and given his reaction, they dared not piss him off further.

"Rise my fellow warriors, and after you find your fucking cocks, sit. It is apparent, I will get no more rest today as we have matters that warrant discussion."

Each of the men stood and made their way to their appointed chair. The men then drew in toward the table, the scraping of wood against the rock floor from the multiple legs of chairs ended their chastisement.

While his family assembled around him, Alaois knew they were not blood born like him, yet would challenge to the death anyone who deemed them harm. With Dagda and Driscoll at his right, Addison and Braden quietly at his left, he glared straight ahead at Stavros. There sat his warriors. *Vamplins*, humans turned vampire against their free will. Those many years ago after they had been turned and forced to battle on the evil side of his race, Alaois found and saved them from their fate of the afterlife. Since then, they were and forever would be his family.

A snide grin stretched across Alaois' hard-edged face as he clapped his hands, rubbing them together. "Now. Who would like to go first? What is so damn important it should disturb my stage of rest?"

CHAPTER TWO

Driscoll, while never timid at expressing his mind, spoke, "We can sense a strange species on the other side. We are not certain of its origin. Yet, we must find out what lies outside our realm." His fist pounded on the table. "I can tell you, I'm not going to fucking sit here until it unearths our domain."

"It's true my lord, "Addison cut in calmly, looking perplexed. "Something is out there; my visions do not tell me which species." His hands stayed folded in front of him on the table, gripped firmly together conveying his concern. After Addison had been turned vamplin, he developed seer power, which came in very handy. At any given moment, he could have a vision. He never knew when they would come. But it was apparent, as he sat disturbed before the men, he'd recently experienced one. Whenever Addison spoke of such premonitions, Alaois took them seriously.

Driscoll wore a determined look as he glared across the table at his leader.

Alaois gave him a lopsided grin. Arching an eyebrow, he turned in his heavy wooden chair, and propped his ass kickers onto the corner edge of the table. Crossing them at the ankles, he leaned back in his chair; arms mimicking his feet as they crossed over his chest. "So eager to catch your prey…eh, D? So quick in fact, you again, forget the sun has a few hours still until it sets behind the sea? Only then, shall we seek out the invader who has foolishly ventured too close to our dwelling."

The rest of the men remained silent as he spoke.

Turning his attention back to Addison, Alaois gave a quick bow of his head. "You did well. Your gifts are never taken lightly with me," he assured him, then returned his attention to the rest of the men. "If whatever is out there is related to the clan responsible for any of your turnings, they will not leave alive. Prepare. We leave at dusk." He removed his feet from the table. "Are we in agreement?" Not waiting for an answer, he finished with, "Good." He slapped his palms against the table, then pushed himself away and stood. "Now that this is settled, I need a drink."

He made his way to the hundreds of wine bottles stacked neatly on their sides, resting inside a room cast by a soft glow from more candlelit sconces located along the walls. One would think they were wine connoisseurs by the large number made available in one place. Only when taking the first sip would anyone's taste buds tell them different. Upon first discovering the cavern, Alaois spent months chiseling sections and tunnels constructing only what was needed for him and his men.

While carving and shaping one of the many rooms, he discovered their imminent resolution. A location kept securely hidden. If someone looked hard enough, behind the mountain of glass bottles, they would discover a small hole in the far back corner. Inside, revealed the key element of their survival. An opening exposing a rare assortment of ice crystals; translucent gems of a lustrous oval shape found in all sizes. Inside each gem, a liquid could be found, resembling the equivalent of drinking water. Yet, it was anything but.

Over time, this one facet helped wean Alaois' men from the cravings of human blood. He'd heard about such gems, but as centuries passed, it became a myth. Known as the gems of life, they were created by the gods themselves. There were those who believed the gems could bring youth and health to those who drank the liquid from within. However, stories were told of how they were once given to witches or those deemed immortal. Direct consumption of the liquid itself was believed to be toxic. Years experimenting with the godly fluids, Alaois detracted the liquid from the gem and while mixed with his own blood, it didn't harm him or his warriors. On the contrary, it healed their sharp cravings and especially aided in the raging blood-lusting state he first found them in. Being a blood born vampire Alaois' blood was the purest of the vampire race.

Inside the hidden section of the cavern where the gems originated, supplied them with millions of doses, and would last them for hundreds of years, if not more. Strangely enough, the more gems Alaois took, the more he found, as they seemed to magically replenish themselves within the walls. So, inside each wine bottle, contained several cups of liquid from the ice crystals combined with a few drops of Alaois' blood. In the years they took refuge in the cavern, they'd stocked hundreds of bottles.

Although, Alaois could go without consuming the mixture, his men being vamplins, would forever require such consumption. He wished he could share his discovery with others of his kind who hoped to aid other vamplins. However, if word of such gems were found, it would bring forth vampire clans who wished the blood cravings of vamplins not to be tamed. Those wanting vamplins to run free and corrupt the human race. It would start a war and Alaois couldn't risk it…not now.

Over time, he'd even discovered the gems aided his men if any were critically wounded. The godly powers of the liquid would rejuvenate and strengthen their bodies and even his own, allowing them to heal quickly; making the secrecy and security of its discovery of paramount importance.

Removing a bottle from its resting place, Alaois pulled at the cork with the tip of his fangs until it popped free and then spit it onto the floor. Lifting the glass bottle to his lips, he drank, consuming the gut quenching life force. Eyes closed, he allowed the vitality of the liquid to distribute through his veins. It's been over a year since his last drink and knew he would need the energy if he did in fact face such clans. For years, they made the hidden caverns beneath the inlands off the Sea's of Marmara their domicile, and he would be damned if anyone was going to come ashore to disrupt and harm his men.

Although, he didn't particularly need the gem's liquid to ease his blood cravings, it somehow affected his body differently than his men. After consuming its known healing powers, every cell in his body tingled and he felt stronger in a way. More powerful and robust. He welcomed the energy it gave him and today, he would be ready for whatever lingered outside their realm.

Standing with his back to the doorway, palm leaning against the wall supporting his massive frame, he consumed the ice crystal fusion. Because of his keen hearing, Alaois heard Stavros approach behind him. Opening his eyes, he ran his tongue along his bottom lip and turned slightly to the left to glance at his warrior from over his shoulder.

"My lord." Stavros bowed his head in respect.

"Speak what is on your mind, Stavros," Alaois prompted, then leaned forward to put the empty bottle back in its place.

"What do you think is out there? Could it be one of the clans have returned after learning of our location?"

Alaois grunted. "No. I don't believe that to be true. My senses tell me it's none we have ever known. I cannot lock onto the species either."

With obvious respect, Stavros dipped his head. "My lord." He then turned on his heels.

About to walk away, Alaois spun around and clasped the back of Stavros's shoulder. "The day when the clan does find us, they will die. Mark my words." Fully aware of the weighty thoughts going through his warrior and most esteemed friend, Alaois stood with a heavy heart, watching as Stavros walked away.

Not saying a word, Stavros left with a mere nod of his head.

CHAPTER THREE

When Alaois sensed the sun receded enough not to be of threat to him or his men, he guided the way through the tunnel. He navigated the one passageway leading up to ground level from the depths of their cavern quarters that rested more than twenty feet below the earth.

The rays of the gods' sun to a vampire were their deadliest weakness, a vulnerability that would instantly turn them to ash and send them onto the afterlife. Whether one of birth born or vamplin, they were for eternity what the gods deemed— the soulless. Soulless monsters of the night the humans called vampire or blood-sucker. Nonetheless, Alaois remained damn proud of who he'd been born to be and although soulless, he and his men were every bit as vigorous and indistinguishable as the gods.

Vampires possessed the same immortality and even the same strength as the gods. Yet, the gods cursed vampires who prevailed on earth and so they willed humans to hunt and destroy them. The result left vampires angry and rebellious toward all humans, and therefore, created vamplins to beseech and kill any human who crossed their path.

Alaois and his men were not in accordance with such punishment toward the humans. It was the gods who created chaos between the two species. Vampires such as him and his men chose to remain unseen for they would not condone war amongst neither the humans nor their own. Thus, being the way they'd lived for centuries.

Of any of the men, Alaois had more reason than not to hate the humans. His father was killed by a human hunter. Many centuries ago, after his father's death, Alaois decided to go off on his own, in search of the human who sent his father onto the afterlife. During the time of his journey, he crossed paths with the men who ended up being his loyal and most esteemed family.

He first discovered Addison, Braden and Dagda who just days before were turned vamplin, left to survive only for no more than shits and giggles. It enraged him.

Knowing from that day forth, they were to be submissive to the ones who turned them and even more so to those birth born. Birth born vampires were the oldest of the vampire hierarchy, having been born into the life of the blood fanged creature, not turned from another. They reigned and were the strongest, and most respected above all others.

Alaois detested clans who created vamplins, only to use them to hunt and kill humans, or leaving them to fend for themselves, thus risking the exposure of their race. He'd taken in Addison, Braden and Dagda from a clan who left them blood lusting in the alleys of Chicago, in the U.S.

Driscoll and Stavros were another story. They were vamplins who were courageous fighters, lethal warriors among the vampire clan who turned them. Alaois had stopped to feed in an old village off the Turkish border, and sensed two vampires fighting humans. The pair of human males had waited outside in an alleyway and jumped them for making advances toward their human women in a local pub. Little did they know the vamplins knew of their plan and took full advantage of the situation. Alaois could sense they were on the verge of blood bingeing.

The darkened alleyway would have been perfect for what they were after. But

Alaois broke up the fight before the humans ended up sitting in their own blood baths, and quickly mind fucked them to get as far out of town as they possibly could. The two vamplins had convincingly hidden their hungry red eyes from the humans by wearing shades. Alaois had spotted their black sunglasses broken on the red brick street.

"Do you idiots really think you can continue this reckless behavior and not risk exposing yourselves?" Alaois shouted.

"What's it to you, pop?" Driscoll retorted. Even then, he never could hold his tongue.

The other vamplin stood silent, a hard look on his face.

"I can offer you much more than the life you are living now."

"We were doing just fine until you came along. Now you've ruined our mission." Driscoll snarled.

"What mission?" Alaois asked, though he knew already.

"Those humans were to go back with us. You will pay once our leader hears what you've done."

Alaois detected fear in Driscoll, despite his arrogance appearance. "I know who you both are. The humans would not have made it alive. You would feed on them until they were dead. You are vamplins. The cravings would overpower you both and blood would be all you could think about until it took you over."

"You know nothing!" the other one finally spoke.

Alaois liked Stavros from the beginning. He reminded him so much of himself. Stubborn, arrogant, fearless. A true warrior. "So, you do have a voice after all."

"I'm Stavros. Leave now, or it will be *you* we take back to our leaders."

"You can try, but it will not be that easy. Come with me and I can show you both a better life than this. A future where you control your cravings and will never again, be controlled by those who think you worthless."

Hisses came from both, apparent they didn't care too much for being called 'worthless'.

"Did you know once your clan discovers you have lost your control of blood cravings, you are no longer of any use? They will destroy you and then go out and turn more humans into vamplins?" He paused and waited. Alaois could tell his words were making sense to them.

Neither vamplin moved.

"That is too bad." He took a step back and turned to leave.

The quieter of the two spoke, "Do not do us any favors."

Nonetheless, they both followed him.

He knew they were of no threat and took their silence as their answer. It was by choice they followed him, not by submission. Taking in the men, he taught them the proper way to survive their destiny. To take control of their blood lust and taught them a life where they and humans could co-exist. They didn't need to kill to survive.

Since that day, they pledged their eternal life to him, and of the five, Driscoll and Stavros grew the closest to Alaois. However, a moment didn't go by when they were not haunted by their violent killings of innocent humans before Alaois showed them a better way.

In those years, the men also came into their own powers and became very useful to Alaois. Stavros and Driscoll's powers allowed them to erase memories. They often used it when they ventured into the states for supplies; erasing any memory from whomever they crossed paths with, ensuring their secrecy.

Alaois, at times, would call upon them when needing to aid humans who struggled with the same fate after being turned. Those who couldn't grasp their new vamplin life, Driscoll or Stavros would enter their mind stripping the entirety of their human years. At first, it took a toll on both of them. Reliving the past days of their turning was difficult, but coming to grips with what they did seemed better than death. With their job complete, Alaois would summon a birth born of another clan, so the vamplin could be taken in and shown the right path.

The powers of the other three, Addison, Dagda, and Braden's were each different.

Addison would have visions, yet not of the past or future. Limited only by the present, in which supplied them with a small window of warning. This restriction to present time occasionally caught them off guard, not allowing them enough time to act. This pissed Alaois off, but there was little they could do about it...only to use it best to their advantage.

Dagda's ability held the power of technopathy, a skill to manipulate technology. Noticeable as a special form of electrical/telekinetic manipulation, it allowed him to physically interact with machines. A psychic ability allowing him mental interface with computer data from anywhere in the world. He controlled objects by using his mind in ways not visible to the naked eye, very convenient with regards to their cash flow.

Braden on the other hand, was gifted with the skill of mind control. Not able to erase the minds of others like his fellow warriors, Driscoll and Stavros, yet he could change the course of a thought. What a person may have thought they heard or saw, he could switch to something different altogether.

One day, Dagda and Braden materialized from the depths of their cavern to a town, miles away. In need of materials, the humans from the small village didn't welcome their visit. Quickly purchasing their items, and while exiting the store, Dagda and Braden were confronted by an angry mob. Guns and pistols gripped in the hands of human men encircled around them. Neither Dagda nor Braden attempted to move from the store's front entrance.

As told by Dagda later, the corner of Braden's mouth slowly rose in a witty grin. Concentrating, he lowered his eye-lids and pushed his powers among the mob, entering their minds. He replaced the thoughts of attack with thoughts of them gathering in preparation for a hunting excursion, changing their temperaments of hatred toward them to excitement for a deer hunt.

Later, after Dagda and Braden returned home, they boasted and laughed about their clever trickery. But they meant the humans no harm.

One thing was certain. Alaois dared any human, or immortal to try and stand in any of his men's way. Honored and fucking proud to lead them, he would forever hold his vow of eternal loyalty till he joined his ancestors in the afterlife.

Only when other birth born vampires beseeched Alaois, did he venture out from their dwelling in order to aid those in need of his help. In spite of that, their survival rested on keeping themselves hidden from all humanity and other vampire clans. When and if the time came when they were discovered, he and his men would be ready.

CHAPTER FOUR

Continuing along the tunnel passageway from their cavern, they stopped at a stairway dead-ending at another tunnel channeling up. Once the men climbed the more than thirty-foot high steps they each treaded out, yet still remained hidden inside a darkened cave. Dagda sealed the access of the tunnel with a boulder. "This damn thing seems to get heavier every fucking time!" he huffed.

They were above ground, but the cave kept the main opening to the tunnel hidden.

"Oh, stop your complaining, D. You sound like a human." Braden laughed.

After Dagda flipped Braden the bird, they continued the few feet left before the cave exposed them to the outer world. Each of the men gazed upward at the night's star salt-sprinkled sky. The bright white specks blazed like each one individually led the way to a different passageway above the heavens. A place none of their kind would ever set eyes upon.

The vamplins ventured off in different directions searching for any signs of life. Stavros, Addison and Braden climbed over the cave's sharp, edgy, rock-covered exterior and headed inland toward the woods. Driscoll and Dagda headed left, to hunt along the beachfront.

Before the warriors disappeared, Driscoll called out, "If I get to them first, and for what I have in store for them, there will be nothing left for your sorry asses!" Licking his lips, he wiggled his eyebrows followed by his annoying laughter as it rang into the dark.

The men rolled their eyes at his tantalizing ways.

Alaois shook his head at Driscoll and commenced his search alone, as he preferred. Heading in the only direction remaining, east. Birth born vampires possessed an array of powers and he'd trained his men to utilize their vampire-side, so they could have a sixth sense of mind interaction. The men couldn't enter one another's minds to read their thoughts like Alaois could, yet they did have the ability to send mental brainwaves between the six of them with a simple thought.

Wandering along the smooth white sands of the Marmara Seas, Alaois noticed a trail of moonlight shining along the crystal sands lighting his travels. He glanced behind him and watched his men disappear, sending a mental, *stay alert and don't be careless.*

Then turning back around, he noticed how the moonbeams accentuated his size elevens footprints. The wet sunken imprints in the sands as he walked made him unintentionally smile at their ironical message. The left behind footprints truly represented the very creature making them. One who struggled at surviving, always trying to avoid being washed away; swept to an afterlife of darkened seas.

The hour warm and the salty air thick, Alaois continued his stride, the only sounds came from the ocean waves as they invaded the shore. Water white capping as it rushed in, smacking firmly against the sides of his boots, splashing upward on the pant legs of his jeans. The sea desperately tried to obstruct his passageway, unable to succeed.

Moving closer inland would have been the obvious thing to do, but he couldn't get himself to move away from the direction his feet guided him. The sea tide approached closer at his left, while a long line of dark woods stood mysteriously to his right. The farther he walked, the faster the ocean waves moved in, crashing up against the side of his body more forcefully.

Lost in apprehensive thought for the safety of his men, Alaois suddenly caught a scent off in the distance. Stopping dead in his tracks, he inhaled deeply trying to lock on the species. It came from the inland of woods. Catching him so off guard, a huge wave came charging up and scooped the bottoms of his feet out from under him, picking his huge frame off the ground and ass planting him hard on the not-so-soft sands below.

Turning his body onto his side and glancing toward the woodland, he propped up on his knees, resting his hands on the tops of his upper thighs then squeezed his eyes shut. Slowly, his head moved in a half circle motion and he took a deep inhale of breath, again trying to catch the scent. *Female...human.*

With astonishment at his discovery, Alaois' eyes popped wide-open and he leapt to his feet. Bending at the waist, he tried to brush off the wet sand glued to his jeans. Gritty grains stuck at once on the insides of his palms and fingers, infuriating him to no end. He cursed and scanned the woods, again catching the female's scent. It was stronger. A coconut and citrus fragrance ran up his nostrils and through his body, revving his senses into overdrive. Humans were the enemy and nothing but food.

However, he became perplexed by his body's reaction to the human's scent. The strong heady perfume made him for the first time, crave the days of the sun. Was this what summertime smelled like? Humans *never* had an odor other than the claim of prey. This didn't make any fucking sense! It made him even more intrigued to find her and see just who this woman was.

While he examined the area with his heightened sight, strands of his shoulder-length dark black hair blew across his face. The winds picked up and a spark of lightning flashed off in the distance followed by a crackling roar. Tops of trees bent by violent winds from a raging thunderstorm approaching from the west and with great speed. The approaching rain quickly replaced the female's scent.

Balling his fists, not wanting to leave, Alaois knew he needed to gather the men before the storm hit. Once the storm came, the raging thirst of the sea's tide, would make the ocean waters cover the entrance to their cave. They could swim underwater and reach the entrance, yet the vast waters would keep the boulder forcefully pushed against its opening. Even the strength they contained could not withstand the forces of the sea.

Just as Alaois pivoted his body, the female's scent caught him, again. He couldn't fight it. The intoxicating aroma caused friction in the lower region of his body, surprising the hell out of him. An aching, now throbbing cock concealed deep inside his jeans now awoke after centuries of sleep, raising its head in full recognition. A domineering rush of desire pushed a growl through his throat.

His conscience be dammed as the greedy bastard pushing against his zipper told him to go. Seek her out. Alaois did just that. His feet took off in a dead run, heading straight into the darkest part of the woods.

CHAPTER FIVE

Bolting past thick green branches and tree trunks at a vampire's supernatural speed, Alaois swatted through the broad and narrow leaves and stems with his hands, determined in clearing any obstacle in his path. Hearing something off in the distance as a twig snapped, causing him to whip around in a flash of a second. His throat closed. *MINE!*

An exquisite woman stood before him, draped in a platinum gown that outlined every curve of her body. Long strands of pale white hair sparkled like diamonds as they fell in fluid waves past her waistline. Some locks were teased by the winds causing them to cover her succulent breasts.

Alaois growled at their disrespectful placement shielding her perky mounds of flesh straining against the thin fabric. His hands suddenly craved to reach out, remove all that hid the beauty underneath to caress with his palms that which he achingly desired.

With a lustful gaze, his eyes drifted to meet hers and h*oly fuck*; he stared directly into a pair of translucent pearl-like eyes. Every section of his monstrous frame froze as they stared at one another. Every muscle in his body tensed. Trying to find his voice, all the while, his mind screamed inside his head.

MINE…Take her…she is yours…why do you hesitate?

Then his cock, damn it to hell, throbbed violently inside his jeans from its confinement. It pleaded to be released and introduced to her core, as quickly as possible. Swallowing hard, he tried to regain his self-control.

He needed find some kind of inner gallantry, being rusty on the treatment of a beautiful female who shockingly provoked something raw within him. A feeling unusual and most unexpected, for no female in his lifetime had affected him in such a way. "My name is Alaois. What is your—" He suddenly felt unable to continue when a feverish swell of the glands inside his mouth and throat exploded from a much stronger scent coming from her…*Blood!*

What the fuck? Moving his gaze toward this mouthwatering aroma, Alaois spotted the blood. On the inside of her arm, a large cut bleeding out from its binding. His whole body began to quiver. The bloodlust rose within him to take what flat out invited him over into temptation. Grinding his teeth, Alaois had to hold his breath, for any moment his body and mouth could easily seize this female prey, fully consuming what now seemed to be graciously offered before him.

While she would be nothing but food to others, his instincts told him so, yet all his senses shouted, *Mine. Protect!*

He raged a battle to hold himself back, fearing he would hurt her. Alaois collapsed on his knees at her feet. He brought his hands up covering his face, shielding his exposed fangs and shouted for her to run. Perceiving her feet moving closer toward him, he did the only thing he could do. Alaois removed his hands from his face, glared up at her locking his pained gaze with her innocent one and bared his fangs. He roared out in a hiss of hunger, "I. SAID. RUN!"

Panting, Aretha ran through the woods until her feet could carry her no further after the male yelled *run*. The one she sensed approaching her within the hidden trees of the forest turned out to be a vampire. *How fascinating.*

Glancing down at the crook of her right arm, blood ran from the make-shift bandage she fashioned earlier in the morning from torn strands of her gown. To heal a gash she'd received from one of the hunter's arrows. She stood frozen while the effects of her wound resulted in the vampire's eyes to dilate.

His expression had instantly changed to a hungered crazed animal.

Somewhere inside of her, guilt struck for having inflicted pain on him. Had she known he was vampire, she would've never allowed him so near. Yet, when their gazes locked, her heart pumped and fluttered, pushing against her chest. Was it fear or anticipation? Something inside wanted her to proceed closer until their bodies touched. However, a curse lingered over her like a plague in hopes of destroying all she encountered. So, because of her curse, she'd remained in place.

Aretha smiled now at how the vibrant moonbeams peered down casting its pale light around this vampire's massive frame.

His immense muscular build elevated him like a god of darkness. Hell, he probably was a god. Inspecting him, she took pleasure in how his black tee wrapped such delicious muscles and were tucked firmly into the top of his wet sand-covered jeans, which made her smirk with curiosity. The thin cotton fabric of his shirt showcased fine lines of thick rippled abs.

Aretha bit her lower lip while remembering the way they pushed out against the tightness of the shirt like powerful waves of water. She nervously gazed up along his chest and outwards at his arms, they were like huge round mounds of coconuts concealed by flesh. His powerful build completed the godly specimen of the man he appeared to be. Finally stopping at the vampire's face, she tilted her head.

No doubt, this bold man probably endured centuries of battling for survival. His hard and firm features made this obvious. He never altered his inquisitive expression though, as those dark eyes never removed their gaze from her.

Her eyes had lingered on his five o'clock shadow, ridged around his defined jaw line. Then—oh, dear God, gusts of westerly winds blew in and snuck through his fine silk strands of hair causing him to fork his fingers through in hopes of keeping them away from his face. As if in slow motion, the rich and more erotic shades of dark chocolate tresses blew loosely across his tanned face matching the beautiful irises staring back at her.

No doubt, this vampire was lethal and certainly dangerous, but he stirred a craving and a desire she wanted to explore in every possible way.

While admiring his overwhelming physique, a pulsating throb came surprisingly not from her heart, but at her core. The sensation almost dropped her to her knees. Her breasts constricted against the fine white silk of her gown aching to be handled and kissed by the hands and mouth of this vampire.

Hungry for his tempting lips, hers parted and she sighed at the thought of what he could probably do with her body. Yet, should she even contemplate such a thing? Was she thinking rational? This male was a vampire, he drank blood to survive. Was she falling for his trickery to reel her in as his prey?

For so long, Aretha prayed to feel the way many goddesses from Olympus spoke about, yet she never experienced such an emotion, and had longed for the day. What she didn't expect was the desire for one of the damned. This would really go well in

Olympus, she rolled her eyes at how they all would react to such a thing.

For months now, Aretha spent her days and nights on these sandy beaches and never once came across anyone other than animals from the woods…At least, until recent events. With her guard down, she foolishly transformed out in the open where human hunters witnessed her. Now having exposed her curse, they hunted her.

Yet, didn't vampires ambush their prey in order to consume its blood? Wasn't that their fundamental nature? So why, when this vampire looked at her, full of agony, did he demand she run to seemingly keep him from harming her? It didn't make sense.

Releasing a sharp breath at the vampire's reaction, Aretha recalled how her day started. It compared to no other and certainly would go down as the most eventful of days she'd encountered since her years of being cast down to the earth.

Earlier that morning, she'd been in mid-flight, enjoying the nice cool breeze as she soared above the Black Sea. She finally discovered the location, a place which eased the sadness of the curse her body involuntarily transformed into at each sunrise.

The warm, fresh air and bright cobalt-blue sky lifted her spirits, and while galloping through cumulus clouds, an arrow rocketed past her ear. Then seconds later, she heard the sound again, yet this time, an arrow struck her from out of nowhere. Forcing her descent, she crashed onto the wet damp wooded forest along the coastline of the Sea of Marmara, south of the Black Sea…

Then soon after, she met the alluring and unforgettable Vampire God.

CHAPTER SIX

Aretha frowned now as she bent over, ripping another section of silk from the bottom of her gown. Then, she snatched up a few vines scattered around her bare feet. She covered the silk cloth over the blood soaked one and wrapped it several times with the vine, tying it tightly over the crease of her arm. It'd been a long time since she felt pain of any kind. Being mortal would take some getting used to.

Life had changed, and all because she refused a god.

Far beyond the stars, Aretha once lived on Mount Olympus. A goddess loved and worshiped by all, she always found sanctuary sitting at a fountain centered amongst an array of multicolored gardens. Birds chirped and sang their love tunes as they flew by while others perched on cherry blossoms or pink and white dogwoods circling the grounds.

Aretha's favorite place rested among millions of flowers. Their invigorating perfumes engulfed one's senses with every type of bloom crafted by the gods. A place of absolute bliss and serenity. She spent most of her time in the gardens, centered in the middle of their holy temple. Known as the Goddess of Soul, her eyes were only able to see those who beheld their living spirit, such as humans, or those of the righteous and worthy. Those presumed soulless were deemed as evil. Damned and not for her untainted eyes to look upon. Therefore, she'd yet to see such a species.

Other than the damned, Aretha could gaze down through the clouds, and search out the righteous mortal humans who inhabited the earth. While watching, she always inhaled the sweet aroma of the many blossoms around her with their limitless colored blooms, they never lost their brightness from their newborn petals.

She spent her time in the same place where Neptune, God of the Sea, would appear usually without notice. Those were the gods for you...Never did they feel their approach needed forewarning. Neptune sought Aretha's location whenever he damn well pleased. He also happened to be in love with her.

Any other goddess would've been honored to be held in such high regard. Aretha on the other hand, couldn't stand him. His advances sickened her.

Each time, he would slowly walk up in his regal white robe, displaying his distinguished white beard, his Trident always in hand. Trailing one finger down the length of her arm, he would remark at how soft her skin felt. Leaning in while whispering promises of seduction.

Unwanted promises which she chose to block out.

Neptune would be unaware of how she cringed whenever he gazed at her. Till one day, he came to her while she sat quietly on the edge of the white marble fountain.

She'd been tracing her fingertips along the top of the cool water, and smiled at the multi-colored Kio fish swimming in the small pool. The same crystal clear waters twirled around a stone statue of Zeus. From the middle of his marble chiseled lips spouted water in a spray which traveled back into the waters below.

Kneeling down on one knee in front of her, Neptune took Aretha's hand in his and made his intensions known, presenting her with a vow of eternity. A vow never to be broken and a declaration of the highest honor because it came from a god—one not to be rejected.

Tears streamed down Aretha's face as he remembered the day all too clearly. Aretha slid her hand from his hold, "Please, Neptune. I do not welcome your advances. You should seek another goddess in which to tempt your desires."

Her words angered Neptune and drove him to place a curse on her for refusing him. "How dare you turn away my affections! Do you know the honor in my regard?"

Aretha stood and headed toward the gardens. Turning to look over her shoulder she proclaimed, "Too many times you have come here and made advances. I do not share them. Nor can I stand the touch of your skin on mine. Yes, I understand the regard in your proposal, but you will respect mine." Not only did she refuse his eternal promise, but she degraded him as a god. Aretha would never fail to remember the crazed look in his eyes.

His maddened temper flared as he raised his voice and arms in result of her rejection, lifting the seawaters below the heavens, casting havoc on all the lands at his command.

Thus, the last memory she could recall from her immortal goddess life. The next thing she knew, Aretha woke up on a warm bed of sand. Trying to maneuver her heavy limbs, she panicked after discovering her new body. Her appearance no longer resembled human form. Pure white short fine fur covered her entire body and glancing over at what should've been her human right shoulder only to find—wings.

Tracing her eyes over her new horse figured frame, she gasped in shock, peering down at four hooves and then turning the crest of her neck to find strands of a thick white mane. Lowering her head, Aretha peeked in between her legs, and sure enough, a silvery white tail swished back and forth in the ocean breeze. Tears flooded from her eyes and a voice all too familiar made her jolt straight up toward the bright blue sky.

It came from the one god responsible for her new fate. "Pegasus you are, Aretha. For your defiance, you will remain a Pegasus of the gods during the hours of the sun. When darkness shadows the earth, your body will become a mortal human, defenseless and frail. From this point forward, you can see all species on earth, even the damned, as you are now subject to all creation. For it sickens you to look at me and feel the touch of my godly skin? I therefore, place a curse on you this day. For not only will your body change in the passing of the moons, but just a simple touch of any male, human, immortal or any other living species shall cause you to perish. Your soul is no longer immortal and if death takes you, you will not join us within the heavens. Hell and evil will possess your soul. For this, thou shalt *never* know the power of a man's touch until you renounce your words spoken and join me in the temple."

Then, a female's voice replaced his. Another goddess from the heavens. Adonia, who'd yearned for the affections of Neptune, one with greater power than Aretha, spoke in harsh tones, securing Aretha's fate, "Stupid girl. You will learn never to refuse one as great as Neptune. We are chosen and are never to reject. I would have done anything for Neptune to look at me just once the way he gazed at you. Zeus has been told about your insolence and he concurs with your punishment." Jealous at Aretha's refusal, the goddess' words were filled with hatred as she continued, "May you live with remorse at your new life; for eternity!"

Then silence fell, leaving Aretha on the soils of earth, sobbing—*Pegasus by day, mortal by night.*

CHAPTER SEVEN

Coughing up dry heaves, still bent on his knees, it took everything Alaois had not to pursue the female and take what his body hungered for. The woman instantly and unexpectedly became more of a temptation than he thought he would ever encounter.

Knowing only a few feet separated them and his every whim from having her blood flow down his throat, replenishing and reinforcing every cell. Always able to resist attacking and taking blood from humans before, yet the fragrance of coconut and citrus combined with the essence of her blood, the sounds of her thumping pulse as each vein pumped the mouth-watering enticement lingered like a seductive spirit.

Never in recent years did Alaois struggle with his self-control, until now. Fighting hard against his birth born instincts, he replaced the cravings with images of what his blood-lusting affects would do if he engaged. The grisly vision kept him in place.

Damn it, how could one have this kind of control over him? Not possible. He sensed the female was of human descent, yet an impulse told him there was more to her than she appeared. One secret she kept hidden, leaving him desperate to know more. Except a siren went off inside his head; reminding him that this battle would be for his self-control. Not knowing which, either the blood lusting or the inner craving to take her as his, would be the fight he would struggle against when he gazed at her a second time. This made him want her all the more.

Yes. He would see this human woman again, and soon. *MINE!*

In a mental undertone, Alaois heard his name enter his mind from one of his men's call. Suddenly, he realized the storm had reached the shore. Large drops of rain hit heavy on his shoulder blades as they plummeted from the packed clouds unable to hold their weight any longer.

"Alaois, my lord, where are you? Call me and I shall come." Driscoll beseeched him.

How long had his body remained crouched over in this position? Then, out from the thick brush, he heard his men approach. He sensed them as one by one they drew up behind him. Alaois lacked the courage to look at them. Not while he remained panting, eyes dilated and fangs exposed as if ready for his kill, yet no prey to be found.

A weighty hand rested and lightly squeezed his upper right shoulder. "My lord, the storm is at its peak. We must reach the tunnel of the cavern before the tide conceals the cave's entrance. We found no traces of anything and sunrise is within the hour."

Hearing Stavros' words, Alaois combed his blood-lusting shaky fingers through his hair and leaned back on his legs folded underneath him. Tilting his head at his friends and fellow warriors, he saw the look of panic cross their faces. Ignoring it the best he could, he nodded and got to his feet, leading the way to the cave.

His men followed. The entire walk back to the cave and through the tunnel, Alaois' men aggravated him with questions. Questions concerning what he observed and what caused him to fall onto his knees in anguish.

The only response Alaois gave them came out as an agitated growl. So, they didn't press the subject. Alaois spoke when he was damn well ready, a trait about him they each already learned the hard way.

Once back in the heart of their dwelling, Alaois stormed to his quarters slamming the metal door shut with a thunderous crash.

The sound traveled the length of the hallway and into the center of the cavern as the men congregated. Their heads shot up in unison toward the ceiling as small pieces of plaster fell from its bonding. Curses bellowed into the room from their expressed concerns for their leader.

Addison and Dagda yanked their chairs out from the table and sat down frustrated. Both men rested their black shit-kickers upon the aged wood table before crossing their arms at the chest. Leaning back, they both contemplated their theories.

The others treaded around the room with puzzled brows, pondering what could have caused their old friend and leader to be in such a state of disarray.

"Did you see the look in his eyes?" Braden spoke with a distressing tone, breaking the silence.

"Yeah, and that's not all. Am I the only one who noticed his fangs were fully elongated with an immense expression of blood-lust across his face? Hell, he has always protected us from exposure, yet there he sat, in the open of the woods, crouched down and exposed. In all these years, he's never lost control like that, never!" Driscoll barked the last.

Stavros scuffed the side of his dark goatee with his knuckles and stopped pacing. Staring at his fellow warriors, he declared, "Something caught him off guard. I have seen the look on his face once before. It was just the two of us, trailing the human scent of his father's killers. We somehow, lost the trail unexpectedly. We were so close, yet lost it." Stavros sighed palming the back of his neck, and began rubbing it with anxiety. "Alaois always caught what he sought. Thus that day, our conquest wasn't fulfilled. But as you all know, the murderer's day of retribution came. However, I will never forget the look of agony on his face. The same look we observed this night."

"Well, shit! What do you think he saw out there then?" Dagda asked while looking baffled. "What the fuck do we do now?"

"We wait," Driscoll answered sternly.

"We all know Alaois," Stavros added. His left hand firmly gripped a dagger concealed in its holster attached at the waistline of his black belt. His other hand fingered through his short jet-black hair.

"He does not speak until he is ready. Question him and you may as well talk to that stone wall," he thumbed behind his shoulder, "or you will wake up a week later to find your face distorted wondering what the hell happened. He talks in his own time."

Various tones of agreement were uttered throughout the room. But they knew something happened out there in the woods. The question of what exactly would go unanswered, for now. Then all of a sudden, they heard a piercing roar. Their heads swiveled toward the tunnel belonging to Alaois. They looked at each other and in unison cursed, "FUCK!"

Inside his chambers, Alaois couldn't stop thinking of the mysterious female. On edge, he felt like lit dynamite about to ignite at any moment. How many hours until nightfall? The lengthy age of the sun at its full beam blazing across the earth gave him too long to covet the female. Hands clenched into fists while pacing, all the while, his mind violently screamed *MINE*, repeatedly. Why did he react to her in this way? He didn't know her. A stranger, yet she was more—so much more.

He teetered at the brink of ripping down every stone, rock and grout that kept him bound inside the walls, his need so great, even his men were wary to come near. He could hear them talking, but paid no attention. No need. He knew their discussions were over the scene of him in the woods. Allowing his men to find him in such turmoil added to the fuel already boiling from within. The moment the sun set behind the edge of the sea, he would go in search of her.

Alaois willed to life the man-made grey and black limestone shower. He waited to enter until steam came from the washroom like reams of smoke. Steam triggered by the combination of a mud volcanic streamline and a natural cool spring he and his men tapped into years ago. It supplied them with bathing water.

Stripping off his clothing, he stalked into the vapor-covered shower and tilted his head up under the hot liquid. The pipelines and plumbing were thanks to Dagda. Water trailed down the top of Alaois' head, breaking around his body.

Taking hold of a bar of soap, he and his men made using waxes and oils from surrounding plant life, he palmed it until suds formed in his hands. He rubbed them along his upper biceps and across his chest. Thoughts of the female never left his mind. His body jerked when his head tilted downward and he realized his palm had a firm grip on his cock. Years had passed by since he and the fucker interacted. Those useless encounters of pleasure he gave up on ages ago.

Now with the enticing visions of the female on his mind, his hand, of its own accord, began moving up and down his shaft.

Alaois closed his eyes, letting his head fall back at the enjoyment running through his body. Hot water hitting his upper torso, trailing down the front of his body, the rhythm of his hand increased as he squeezed harder and tighter against his hardened length. Releasing a moan into the steam engulfed room, his body inclined forward and his left palm slammed hard against the stone of the shower wall.

"Yesss...Oh...Fuck yesss!" Visions of the female's pink lips covering his cock, her silvery wet strands of hair slapping against his tight thick thighs while she sucked harder and faster up and down his shaft, and he couldn't hold back the scream as he hit his climax. "Fuuuk!" Hot seed launched, shooting across the shower and down his wrist.

Out of the blue, a sweet scent emerged, mixing into the thick mist and soapy air around him. A saccharine scent having never emitted from his pores in all his years of existing and only emerged when a birth born found their truemate. The claiming scent of the vampire would be the same as the fragrance of their truemate. This made him even angrier.

Inside his palm, his cock stood rock hard surrounded by a coconut and citrus aroma spread as thick as his arousal. Alaois cursed, perceiving the fucker's appetite, and only the female from the woods could satisfy its yearning. This one female destined to be by his side as his truemate, and he didn't even know her name. *Fucking fantastic!*

After removing himself from the shower, Alaois scuffed his head with a white bath towel and tossed it onto his bed. He tugged on a fresh pair of black jeans before choosing a white muscle tee. Stepping into his black steel-toed combat boots, he sat on a wooden bench placed in front of his bed and began buckling them up, when it suddenly dawned on him. *What if she is in greater danger than she was from you? She is your truemate, yet stands unprotected.*

Running his hands along the sides of his head, Alaois became even more perturbed. He yanked at his dark still wet hair and released an endless roar of anger. All the candles in his room flared from his rupture of rage. He then heard heavy footsteps stomping down along the hallway. Sending a mental message to each of his men to stay the fuck away, the sound stopped, indicating they receded at his command.

He didn't have the temperament to deal with them. Too many hours stood in his way. How would he ever survive until then? For the first time, he wanted to kill something to appease the anxiety building inside him. He never thought a female would overpower the lust for blood; yet this one did.

CHAPTER EIGHT

Trotting across the sparkling crystal sands, the bright sun shining upon its surface, Aretha fluttered her mended wing, rejoicing at her healed injury. The warmth of the sun beat down, instilling her with a burst of energy. Expanding her bright-white wings, she stretched like a swan and shot up into the sky. Soaring around the clouds, playing with blue jays and cardinals who gave her comfort, it reminded her of those blessed days as a goddess in the temple gardens of Olympus.

In flight, her knees and hind legs moved gracefully in mid-air. Her feather covered extensions allowed her to glide with free range across the blue skies. While sailing along the scenic afternoon, she smiled at the thought of the vampire she encountered the night before. *I wonder if I will see him again?*

Attention diverted by the vampire occupying her thoughts, an arrow from out of nowhere flew briskly between the middle of her ears. A close miss and it pulled her back to reality. Hearing sharp, she listened while scanning the seashore and spotted four men running down the coastline.

They stopped and one of them pointed directly at her and yelled, "There it is, kill it!" At his words, all four drew their bow and arrows.

Not again!

In unison, they drew back their bows, arrows aimed toward her and then released. The spiked killers soared straight in her direction.

Aretha tried avoiding the sharp-tipped missiles as they whizzed around her, but there were too many. One struck her left wing and the piercing sting made her cry out. Descending toward the earth, twinges of pain ran through her body with each flap of her wing. She aimed toward a thick part of the woods containing some old oak trees. Landing on a thick branch, strong enough to hold her weight with her wings tucked against her sides and tried to listen over the pulsing darts of pain.

With the protection of the night only hours away, it would cast its shadows around her. All she could do now was wait

and hope the fullness of the mature trees
would screen her until then. Strangely
enough, she wished the vampire would
happen to come along and make his
presence known. Although, she still didn't
know if he was friend or foe.

The hours passed and Aretha remained
out of harm's way. The sun defiantly took
its time fading into the endless seawaters.
Somewhat at ease, she drifted down from
the treetop while the soft grass and moss
ticked the bottoms of her bare feet. Standing
now in human form, Aretha's slender
demure frame bore the same silvery gown
that changed with her each night. She turned
her hands this way and that, still in awe at
the manner in which her body transformed
at each sunset.

Wrenching with a nip of pain, she
turned her head and saw a deep gash at the
top left of her shoulder. The three- inch
slash where the tip of the arrow grazed
across her wing still stung with each
movement her body made. The trees saved
her from the day ending much worse. Then a

gurgle of hunger erupted from her stomach, reminding her she hadn't eaten all day.

Hiking through the wooded trails, in search of food, her thoughts were also on the vampire. Not one ounce of fear were in those monstrous eyes. Having only seen him once, and yet she felt no alarm at his presence. Strange. With this being the first time she'd seen one of the damned, Aretha craved to know more about him. Wanted to know why he didn't harm her. To look into those deep dark irises again. This time her mind did linger longer, remembering his other fine features she'd briefly took in at their encounter. Is it possible for one to think about another this much after only such a short time? Why did he intrigue her so?

Still, he remained on her mind. Thick dark hair, muscles that went on for days across his giant beastly frame. Continuing on her way, Aretha brushed loose strands of hair behind her ear. Her thoughts drifted— wondering how his touch would feel. Soft, hard? Did he make love slowly and compassionate, or wild and rough like a crazed brute?

Her heart rate began to increase and she no longer focused ahead. A mirage of him stood before her. The same attire, a thick fabric exposing his arms and shoulders.

What a sight to behold. She ran her arms up the sides and on her tiptoes, brushing her fingers along his shoulder blades. Tight and firm, his tanned skin felt to the touch. She moved in closer. She gasped and closed her eyes as the vampires face leaned down and his lips—

All of a sudden, a sound made her eyes pop wide open. She scanned around but didn't see anything. Panting at the daydream, she took in her surroundings and found a coconut tree, her favorite. After cracking one open and devouring its fruitful juices, she sensed something or someone watching her. Fearful it could be a hunter, she decided she'd better leave and quickly.

Slowly bending down, she placed the coconut on the ground and began to walk ahead. A few strides and her pace grew faster as she heard something close behind her. Whipping around, she gazed at none other than the magnificent vampire.

Silent, the vampire simply stared at her. "You!" she called out, taking a few steps backward. Inexplicably, she felt relieved to see him, and desperately wanted to run up to wrap her arms around him.

Alaois however, just stood there.

"Are you not happy you came across my path again this night, vampire?" she frowned.

"Are you saying YOU are, female?" His tone, dry, yet it still stirred the pool of liquid forming between her legs. His massive iron clad muscled arms were crossed over the chest of his white muscle shirt.

I wonder if he owns anything other than those types of shirts? I wouldn't mind stumbling upon his bedroom for a sneak peak. Come to think of it, I wonder how he lives? Shaking her head, she focused back on his stance.

He hadn't moved an inch. Then all of a sudden, the sides of his mouth formed a grin. "Anytime you wish to see my chambers, all you need is to ask. My name is Alaois and I can show you many things." His smile grew wider.

Oh shit, he heard me?

"Yes. I did." His voice echoed inside her head.

Clearing her throat, her cheeks flushed. She took a few steps forward, bravely closing the gap separating them, yet tried to remain a secure distance. With one hand on her hip, she teased, "Well, I could have used your help earlier. Damn shame you cannot venture into the light of day." Concentrating, she quickly replayed the day's near miss.

"What do you mean?" The fearsomely handsome vampire asked with a forceful tone.

Though his voice was alluring, its rough edge caused her to jump.

"Were you in danger?"

Before she could answer, she noticed him close his eyes and tilt his head upward as though scenting something. She knew he'd found the cut on her shoulder the moment he opened his eyes and she saw they had changed from dark chocolate to fearsome red. Aretha tensed at his reaction.

"Tell me woman, the fresh wound I smell, when did you get it?" Alaois commanded, never taking his hardened gaze away from her.

Not quite sure if his response was due to concern for her injury or the craving for her blood, Aretha took a few steps backward. Creating a good distance between them on the off chance, he lost control, she still didn't know much about him. With the fresh images of those sharp fangs still imprinted in her mind from their first encounter, and now being a mortal human, she couldn't afford the risk. "Hunters," Aretha replied, continuing to pace backwards. "Hunters found me again I'm afraid. I tried to conceal myself but they spotted me flying and—"

"Flying? What do you mean flying?" He barked while stalking toward her.

Aretha started with a jump again, not aware of what she'd said until too late. Still pacing backwards, she smacked into a tree trunk and winced in pain from the wound on her back as it scraped against the rough bark.

Alaois stopped mere inches before their bodies made physical contact.

Aretha now caught a strong scent emitting from him. A powerful hint of citrus and…is that coconut? How strange. Her body reacted like nothing she'd ever experienced. Intense heat rose between her legs and her heart rate increased the longer he stood towering over her. Hell, the vampire was wider than a doorframe. The wetness at her core swelled, proving how ready she was for him but at the same time, she ached knowing she couldn't act on the impulsive yet erotic urge.

"You want me, I can smell you," Alaois huskily whispered.

The heat of his breath, mixed with his stimulating scent, warmed the side of her cheek and ear. This fearsome vampire of a god had her under his mesmerizing spell. Aretha said nothing. She couldn't tell him that with one touch, she would perish. She needed to find a way to fight her longing—and his.

CHAPTER NINE

"I think there is more to you than you are letting on, woman. I intend to learn more. First, what is your name?" he asked.

Aretha stood with her gaze locked on his firm kissable mouth. Her tongue ran along her bottom lip while watching his mouth move as he spoke. The idea came alive in her mind of how their lips would feel pressed softly against one another's. She then forcibly pushed the idea right out of her mind. "I'm known as Aretha, Goddess of Soul. My realm is—was Olympus. Well up until…" Aretha paused and sighed. Could she—should she trust one of the damned? She wanted to, in light of how he made her body want to submit to him.

"Please sit down and talk with me. I would like to hear more about you…please?" Alaois spoke kindly. No hunger remained in his tone as he pulled away from her, and taking hold of the sword attached to his belt, he bent his long well-built legs sitting down in the middle of grassy woods. The redness in his eyes changed back to creamy dark chocolate. Patting the ground beside him, he flashed pearl white teeth as a grin crossed his masculine cheeks.

Returning his smile, she reached inside of herself, grabbing hold of her bravery. Aretha, peeled herself from the bark of wood, and sat a few feet away. Fingers bunched her gown in her hands as she pulled the ripped hem up to her knees and sat, curling her legs under her. Settling down, she released the silk fabric allowing it to swallow around her. Her gaze drifted upwards at the star-covered endless sky and she took a deep breath, exhaling a long sigh and told him everything, "Goddess, yes, I was an immortal among the gods and angels. For my sacred life concluded when I refused a god's vow of his eternity of devotion. A vow I learned should never have been refused."

"Did you love him?" Alaois interjected.

"No." She shook her head, and then turned her gaze toward him. "I did not. When I degraded him with my rejection, he placed a curse on me and sent me down on earth." Aretha noticed Alaois body tensing and the blood-red color of his eyes returned, glaring directly at her.

"If you didn't love him, you made the right choice," he noted his eyes still locked on her.

Nervous, she repeatedly scooped sand in her hand and slowly poured the grains from her fist. All the while, her other hand fiddled with a section of her gown. "Umm, yeah so I thought. But besides being placed on earth, I was also stripped of my immortality and powers. The most significant effect of his curse is as long as the sun shines upon the earth, I will remain in Pegasus form, a winged horse of the gods. At the fall of the sun, I change back into what you see now, nothing more than a mere human, weak as any mortal."

"You should not degrade yourself because of your decision. I can sense the shame you place on yourself. Fear not fair one, for I too have my own curse I live with each day of my existence. I find you courageous and admire your—"

"No…No." Hearing him express his admiration and kindness, Aretha cut him off in mid-sentence. "Alaois, there is more. I'm afraid it will influence your opinion of me once spoken. Words I am afraid of uttering for fear of your reaction."

He reached for her.

Instantly, she yanked away from his touch. "Please let me finish," she replied sadly. Hating to refuse the hand, he so compassionately offered. "A man's touch I cannot receive. For if done so, death shall take me. The god, angry at my refusal, cursed me from contact with any male. So, you see, I will never be able to encounter a man's touch…your touch." Tucking a lock of hair behind her ear, she stared at Alaois, waiting for his response.

His expression looked blank.

Nervously expecting him to get up and leave her to her well-deserved fate, they were suddenly interrupted by voices approaching.

Within seconds, Alaois and Aretha were on their feet. Alaois whispered for her to remain quiet and stay behind him. She didn't argue. Then, he pointed toward a deeper part of the woods and she obeyed, quickly running toward it. Alaois following close behind.

"I think the hunters saw us, what do we do?" Aretha huffed while they ran.

"No harm will come to you, I assure you!" He unsheathed his sword from its holder around his belt. "Only, promise me you will look away. I don't want your eyes to look upon the creature I am," Alaois ordered from behind her.

"You don't scare me," Aretha vowed stopping, she turned to face him, wanting so badly to take his hand in hers and show him she cared.

For a brief moment, they stared at one another like nothing else surrounded them. Then their gazes darted away from one another's and toward the snaps and crunches of branches, indicating the hunters had managed to find them.

Aretha suddenly realized Alaois quietly pointed his sword in the direction of a rock. Quickly, she ran and hunched down the best she could, behind the boulder and peeked out to see Alaois' enormous body engulfed with anger, his fangs elongated and his stance resembling a vicious killer. Right then and there, no matter his monstrous appearance, Aretha's face ballooned in a smile. Vampire, soulless or not, she revered him.

Then not a moment too soon, the hunters came out from the thick brush. All six of them side by side, weapons in hand. All simultaneously pulled back their bows, sharp arrows pointed directly toward him. "Vampire!" One screamed and another right after, "Bonus! You find the horse-woman; I'll take the blood sucker."

Just as they released their bowstrings, Aretha covered her mouth with her fingertips as Alaois took off in a flash of speed and attacked.

CHAPTER TEN

Gasping for air, Alaois lay on his side covered in mud, leaves and all other muck of the earth. In attempt to lift his upper body, he collapsed, as he didn't have the strength. Shifting his head to the side, he searched for Aretha, while trying to catch his breath. Finally spotting her a few feet away, his vision began to blur, coming in and out of darkness and causing him to blink several times to keep her in focus. "She's alive. Good." Whispering a prayer to the gods, he thanked them for her survival.

A sudden pain came from his upper torso. "Aw, fuck," he cursed, lifting his head off the ground and catching a glimpse of what used to be his tanned skin and white muscle shirt, now blood soaked and ripped. Three arrows stuck out from the center of his chest. *Not good.* He was fast, but not fast enough. Blood drained freely from each wound, gliding down the sides of his body.

Alaois' head fell back, hitting firmly against the soil and heard Aretha's footfalls coming toward him.

Watching her collapse onto her knees by his side, he hated how her silk gown tore from the abrupt connection as the ground ripped at the lovely material. He would never forget the worried expression displayed on her exquisite face. Those glassy, tear filled eyes glared at him, her tears instantly swimming at the sight of his condition. When she scanned over his body, it became obvious she didn't know where to attend to him first. He recalled her earlier confession at how she was unable to touch any man. Remorse came over him at how she was cursed and now unable to aid him.

Only yesterday, he'd met this beautiful woman staring at him now and already, she'd stolen his heart which ignited and triggered his scent. The aroma of coconut and citrus engulfed them. Its scent became more than significant to him. When a vampire emitted an odor mimicking that of a female, it signified the arrival of their one truemate. Alaois wanted to confess his devotion for her in this moment and what it meant for the two of them, but in his current state, he couldn't.

"What can I do? Tell me—please!" Aretha cried. Translucent tears fell from her eyes. Gathering the front of her gown, she balled the fabric in her hands as if trying to find a use for them.

Alaois sensed she desperately ached to reach out and help his battered body. He gazed up and painfully met Aretha's forlorn weepy eyes. "You—are safe— all...matters," he mumbled. The number of arrows he'd taken wouldn't kill him, but his body grew weaker due to the loss of blood seeping from his wounds.

Only minutes remained until sunrise and without his strength, he realized he would never make it to the entrance of the tunnel. A problem in fact, that certainly *would* kill him. What he needed could only be found inside his cavern. The one substance he needed and didn't have...the liquid mixture from the ice crystals.

Releasing a long sigh, Alaois swallowed hard, tasting the flavor of his own blood running down his throat from internal injuries. Squeezing his eyes tightly shut in both anger and shame, he realized the line to his life upon earth would be cut too short. He would never risk the lives of his men with the sun's crest so near, so calling for them wasn't an option.

With his right arm lying beside his fragile body, he shifted it slowly across the mud-covered grass near Aretha. "There is something you can—*cough*—do."

Aretha inched her knees closer. Tucking her long white hair behind her ears, she leaned over his body. "Yes? Anything."

"Remove—the arrows—from within my chest. For I do not wish to leave this place…with them intact." Alaois despised having to ask this of her.

Then ever so slowly Aretha carefully placed her delicate fingers on one of the arrows, never uttering a sound, and with tears streaming down her pink flushed cheeks; she began pulling the arrows from his chest.

Alaois tried focusing solely on the daintiness of her porcelain face, as she gripped each arrow with both hands, jerking them out quickly and painfully from their deeply wedged position in his chest and abdomen.

Damn. I—do—love…oh fuck that hurt—this woman.

Gritting his teeth after each pull, he fisted and pulled at strands of grass and mud with each surge of pain. Finally, with the last arrow removed, he peered up at Aretha. Doing his best, he curled his mouth into a smile and in doing so; a trace of blood trickled out and trailed down his chin.

His stare remained on Aretha. Gazing at the beauty he admired above all others, in that moment, he fully accepted the life he'd been dealt. *No regrets.* He would have changed nothing. Regaining his voice the best he could, the blood however making him cough in between raspy words, he avowed, "I wish I could have known—the touch of your skin, the softness and taste of your lips—*cough*...to know what it would feel to wake up with you in my arms. Even in the afterlife, I will crave to have you near, always."

Aretha wept.

Her pitiful sobbing made him ache for her suffering. "Do not cry. You—you gave me the one thing I thought I'd never find." Alaois paused to swallow and as he opened his mouth to continue, more blood rushed from his red-stained teeth and lips. "I'd given up on ever finding you...for centuries—my truemate. Please—*cough*...Tell my men it has been a true honor to be among them. I confer leadership to Stavros. I know he will lead them admirably."

Nearly ready to close his eyes and embrace the welcome of the afterlife once the sun rounded its head over the sea, Aretha jumped from her bended knees and onto her feet. Alaois heard her utter something, but was too weak to catch it. Trying to reach out his hand and ease her anguish, yet even too weak to manage that either. While focusing on Aretha standing above him, a strange look crossed her face.

More tears streamed down her already drenched cheeks. Aretha's attention no longer seemed to be directed at him, but toward the dawn-breaking sky. Next and unexpectedly, Aretha turned and ran, disappearing into the forest.

CHAPTER ELEVEN

Emotions high, Aretha couldn't sit and do nothing with the sun only minutes away. She refused to watch Alaois, a man she was growing to love, to be lost to her forever. While watching him draw closer and closer to death, she again caught the heavenly fragrance emitting from him, circling around them like a mystical perfume. The citrus and coconut calmed and filled her pores, running through her body like a thrilled sexual fantasy.

Take me to the cavern. My men are there. He spoke into her mind. *A few miles west.*

Alaois, too weak, would never reach the safety of the cavern and his men. He needed blood and fast. Without a second thought, Aretha willingly sacrificed her life and offered her own. Yet what he needed to regain his full strength would be more than her body could supply.

That's it!

Aretha leapt to her feet. After removing the arrows and hearing him speak his last words of compassion for her and his men, she could endure his death wish no longer. Even when he mentioned *truemate*, which puzzled her, she knew she couldn't sit there and watch him wait for his un-awakening death. A forever void of darkness, his soulless corpse would pass onto from the heavens. Like hell, she would allow such a thing. Not if she had anything to do about it.

Alaois' blood-drenched body lay helpless before her, the drowning sounds of his cough growing worse. She tasted salty tears sweeping over her lips and knew exactly what needed to be done. Turning away, Aretha whispered, "Please forgive me," and took off in a flat out run. Rushing and tracking through the woods, Aretha had only mere seconds to accomplish the only thing she could to save him.

Arriving at the edge of the forest as it broke off at the sands of the seashore, she didn't stop until her bare feet hit the tides of ocean water. Wiggling her toes in and out of the soupy sands and water, she raised her arms high above her. She slowly lowered her eyes and waited until the very second the tip of the sun began to make its appearance. It seemed like hours. Only in truth, it was less than a few seconds. Heart thumping, it wailed so loud, she swore ships at sea would hear it like a fog-horn from a lighthouse.

When it came, her eyes opened as the round sphere of the sun with its devil rays, slowly crept up from behind the sea, ready to claim the unholy. *Like hell. Not today you bastard!*

Reaching higher into the sky, Aretha yelled out into the sea, "You placed this curse on me Neptune, God of Sea! Know on this day you shall see the affects of your commands. I bequeath my life for his. Take me this day, for I have finally known love. A love I would never have found without refusing one whom I did not...yes, even a god. I give my vow of life to *HIM*, offer my soul for his and accept the terms of my banishment from the heavens. A sacrifice willingly given by me, Aretha, goddess of the high heavens, and one I shall never regret."

Not a second after she spoke, her eyes drifted toward a figure shaping far off in the Atlantic Ocean. A colossal wave underlined the beginning of dawn's dark blue and purple sky, as it drew closer. Then, an all too familiar form of Neptune manifested. His upper body human, his lower half concealed by the emerald green waters of the sea. His expression fumed. "Do you know the

meaning of the words you utter, Aretha?"
Damnation rang from his voice.

"Yes. I understand them perfectly! You
are the reason I came forth and the one
wasting my time in saving him," Aretha
retorted.

"How dare you speak to me in such a
manner? Did you forget in these years who I
am?" Building his figure bigger and moving
closer ashore, Neptune expressed his
outrage. "Do not worry for that soulless
creature. I have stopped time for the present
until our words have ceased."

Aretha crossed her pale white arms over
her bosom. "If you have come for the
retraction of my words spoken those years
ago, you will NOT hear them. I found the
one whom I love, even if it costs my life."
Aretha glared at Neptune, knowing nothing
he could say would alter her task. "This
should bring great pleasure to you, knowing
the one goddess who deprived you shall see
her end. Whilst I wonder why you even
made the trouble at coming, or do you find it
fulfilling to witness my death?" she mocked
as the hurt cut so deeply, she could hold
back no longer.

"Do you not know what this means?
You are giving up an eternity in the heavens
for one of the soulless—"

"Do not speak of those whom you do not know."Aretha interrupted him, "For the gods may think him soulless, I say he is not! He holds the power of love even though his true spirit no longer contains him. Yes, he must kill to survive from the very humans you created to destroy him. He does what he must to live among the ones who hunt his breed to extinction. This is no different than the mortal humans you create, is it not? Do they not fight for their survival from illness and suffrage of the world you placed them in?" All she'd suppressed before rushed from her lips, "Yet, you create them to seek and destroy those whom you do not understand. I say unto you, how dare *you* sanctify humans when the soulless are no different. And you call yourself a god?"

Tightening his godly jaw, Neptune joggled his pitchfork with aggravation. "You will not address me with such contempt from your tongue—I…" he halted. His expression hardened and changed to a torn façade. Surprisingly, he said no more, only turned and plunged into the sea. The ocean rose with a huge wave of high water, then sank back and resumed its calmness.

Releasing a sigh, having missed her one chance at returning to the heavens, still she felt no regret as to her choice. Then all at once, dawn began awakening, rising from the east, and casting its glimmer of light as the sun resumed its appearance onto the world. This was all Aretha needed. Just a hint of dawn rising would be enough for her body to transform, her intention all along.

Extending and flapping her wings as they extracted from the magnificence of her horse frame, she dug a couple times into the sands with her hoof and took off into flight. Flying over the tops of the trees she pinpointed Alaois and soared down, gracefully landing beside him.

His eyes widened in shock, having his first glance at her in this form.

Hiding her nervousness, she approached him. Easing close enough beside him without causing harm, Aretha bent her knees so her shoulder could rest closely next to Alaois' body. She threw back the crest of her neck, so her long white mane landed on her other side, within grabbing distance for Alaois. Swaying her head up and down repeatedly, releasing multiple snorts, she hoped he would comprehend what she wanted him to do.

By the way Alaois shook his head in denial and cried out, causing him to spew into a spasm of bloody coughs, she knew he fought her plan. How in the hell was she going to convince him to grab hold of her

before the sharpness of the sun's rays
reached him?

CHAPTER TWELVE

When Aretha fled him, Alaois tried to lift his body and go after her, but his injuries were too severe and held him as if chains weighed his body. The minutes he lay there, fucking powerless and exposed, the more he wished his men were close enough, so he could mentally call to them. Yet, he knew they were within the safety of the cavern and the distance prevented him from reaching them. Plus, he'd become too weak. *Where was Aretha?* Her sudden and abrupt departure worried him. What if there were more hunters hiding, waiting to attack?

Alaois cursed and then suddenly heard a flailing noise coming from above. His gaze shot upward and in the backdrop of the deep blue and pink dawning skylight, an enormous white Pegasus descended straight for him, and landed elegantly by his side.

"Nooo, Aretha... Noooo!" he roared, spewing blood from his mouth. The upset sent him into a fit of coughs. His head crooked to the side while he still hacked up blood. He gaped and studied each and every inch of her new appearance while she strutted closer. There wasn't a blemish of color other than the angelic white fur and feathered wings; damn those colossal wings. Strong and vibrant as they stretched out exceeding the length of her glorious frame, amazing.

Aretha approached, lowering her muzzle slowly till inches separated his face from her mane and their eyes met. Even though hers were no longer human, Alaois knew his truemate stared back at him, unveiling more love in those two crystal white eyes than he ever thought he deserved.

When she flipped her silvery white mane to the other side of her neck, closer to within his reach, her body language pleaded with him to grab hold. Yes, dawn approached, her transformation more than confirmed the fact. There was no doubt the plan she'd conceived included flying him to the safety of his cavern, yet at what cost to her?

He couldn't allow it. For with one contact, it would kill her. "I will not let you risk your life…for mine. Go! Leave me to my death. Please, Aretha—Go! I do not wish your eyes to see me once the sun claims me," he asked.

A loud grunt came from Aretha's nostrils, then in a movement so quick, she dipped her head and tucked her neck under his back, swinging his body over and onto hers.

"Nooo!" he screamed into the silk strands of her mane. The front of his body pounded hard against her as she leapt into the air. It caused him to gasp for breath from the pain it inflicted as he took a tight hold of her long white tresses.

She flew higher and higher, staying at the tips of the trees, trying hard to avoid as much of the sun the best she could. While in flight, she jerked her head signaling where to take him.

Alaois, in that moment, wanted to let go and drop to his death in regrets of her sacrifice for him. Then the sun's heat already burned his skin, once its full sphere set high on the earth, his body would singe and turn to ash. With the excruciating charring of his skin, and right before he passed out, Alaois pointed toward the direction of the beach where she would find the entrance to the tunnel which led to the cavern.

Throwing an empty glass bottle against the stone wall, its shattered pieces falling to the ground, Stavros massaged the back of his neck with one hand while the other swept across his mouth wiping the blood he consumed. Frustrated and worried, he said, "The break of day is nearing, damn it. Where the fuck is he?" He paced back and forth in the main gathering area of the cavern.

Driscoll walked up and tried to ease Stavros' tension by putting his hand on Stavros' shoulder.

He jumped from his reach before he made contact. "Do. Not. Spit out words on how he will be fine, D. For you and I know he has never risked such closeness of returning before first light. I tell you…something is fucking wrong!" Stavros barked into Driscoll's face. "We should have gone with him, regardless of his orders," Stavros continued.

"And have our asses fed to us for dinner, fucking hell no!" Dagda retorted.

The others sat quietly around the long rectangle table watching Stavros come unglued while forking fingers through his hair. They were all worried for their leader.

Suddenly, all the men's heads jerked at a thunderous pounding noise coming from the tunnel leading to the upper grounds.

"ALAOIS!" Driscoll shouted.

All together, the men charged through the tunnel. A stampede of heavy boots splattered vast amounts of water down the already wet passageway.

Stavros led the way. Reaching the metal doorway, he gripped the handle with all his strength cracking the door ajar. The length of the tunnel sheltered them enough from the sun. The door squeaked as he pushed it open.

All the men gasped at the sight before their eyes.

A white magnificent horse stood tall, radiant and—*Shit.* It wasn't just a horse, but a Pegasus—and on its back, was an unconscious Alaois. The Pegasus stomped its hoof numerous times against the ground before carefully lowering its head followed by its neck and legs. Hunkering its stance to a bow, and ever so slowly, continued downward till it rested on its flank. Next, the white godly creature slid one of its wings across the sand and rock-covered soil and Alaois' body glided down its feathers, gently ending at the ground before their tunnel doorway.

Stavros stared at the breathtaking creature as it rolled his leader onto the floor of the cave. He'd heard about such rare creatures, and stories were told they were animals of the gods. Why would one be so close to their dwelling and why in the hell did it have his leader?

Just as he made an attempt toward Alaois, the Pegasus burst into a tremor of hysteria. A piercing cry erupted from the beautiful mare as it swiftly rose on its back hind legs reaching high into mid-air with its front legs. Landing back on all four hooves, the Pegasus started nudging Alaois' rigid body.

Stavros ever so slowly advanced forward and raised his palm up toward the Pegasus. "Do not fear brave one; for he is alive…thanks to you." Stavros inched the rest of the way toward Alaois' burnt body, then took hold of him from under his arm and tossed him over his shoulder. Carefully hurrying back to the tunnel, he handed him over to the men.

They pulled him inside and disappeared down into the depths of their cavern.

With anticipation at aiding his leader, Stavros paused at the doorframe before leaving and looked over his shoulder, smiling at the winged mare.

It pawed the ground with its hoof, tossing trails of rock and sand behind it. Then heaved its head up and down while snorting.

"I will forever be in your debt for the service you have done for my lord. I thank you—for all I am, I thank you." Stavros placed his hand over his soulless heart and pledged his life to the marvelous white Pegasus with a bow of respect. Then with haste, he closed the tunnel door to close out the oncoming sunlight.

CHAPTER THIRTEEN

The heaviness of his eyes caused Alaois to blink several times while trying to register the lights flickering around him. Propping himself onto his elbows, he tried lifting his upper body.

A hand palmed against the top of his collarbone stopping him from advancing. "Rest my lord, your strength has not yet restored."

Hearing Stavros' voice, it all gradually came back to him. Alaois bolted upright, despite the protests he heard from Stavros or the screams coming from his insides. Peering down at what surely caused the stiffness at his mid-section, he noticed, from his waistline to his armpits, his torso was completely wrapped in white plaster taping. Throwing his legs over and across the bed, he instantly pushed himself entirely off the bedding. Yet, the moment his feet hit the floor, his massive beef of muscle leaned forward, gravity pulling him toward the cold stone.

Stavros' arm instantly caught him. One hand at Alaois' waist, his other shoulder tucked under the pit of his arm; doing his best to lead him back to bed.

"I have to go to her. She is fucking dying! Because of me—she is dying," Alaois wailed.

"My lord, it would kill you to exit the tunnel. The sun's light is at its highest on the other side," Stavros replied calmly.

"Go after her. I command you, Stavros…GO. AFTER. HER." Alaois swayed, ranting as if out of his mind.

Stavros still tried to guide his friend toward the mattress. "My lord, I would with my life go and help the female you speak. But, you know I cannot. You need to drink. Your strength is what you must focus on for now…please, my lord." Stavros' words were full of concern for his leader.

Alaois' weakened body caused him to collapse against his confidant as he finally allowed him to lead his frail body back onto the bed. He surrendered and with the aid of the warrior, rested his neck and back against the pillows comfortably positioned alongside wooden headboard.

Noticing several glass bottles sitting on his bedside table, it appeared some of their corks were already removed and contents empty. He leaned over, one hand firmly on his bandages, and while holding his breath from the twinges of pain, he took one of the unopened bottles.

Stavros rushed to his side and removed the cork before he had the chance.

Alaois stared darkly at his friend while lifting the bottle and drinking its contents.

After guzzling down several bottles, he closed his eyes, thinking of Aretha's lifeless dead body. The white pain the visions caused, burned across his mind. He owed her his life for her sacrifice. At the very brink of darkness, he would find her and give his truemate a final tribute his kind gave to ones lost.

Extensively staring at the closed entrance of the tunnel long after one of Alaois' men left her with nothing but her awaited fate, a part of her hoped Alaois would burst through the door and prove he survived. The painful fact of not knowing might just kill her before the curse did.

Trudging away from the depths of the cave, she knew she would never live to see if he endured another day. The length of her wings dragging at her sides made a grieving trail along the sand. Feeling the hot summer day beat down on her white fur, she didn't fight the tears as they rushed from her saddened eyes. *Come. Take me, I'm ready,* she mentally called to the gods.

Without warning, the voice of Neptune spoke from the sky, "You surprise me, Aretha. For thou does not seem happy. Was it not you who chose this sacrifice?"

I'm not discussing this with you. Just do with me what you came here to do, Aretha mentally replied as a single teardrop snaked its way down along the side of her short furry cheek.

Dost thou think I enjoy what is demanded of me now? You are responsible for what I must do.

What I did, I did for him and will never regret my decision. When you send me to my death, know my last thoughts will be of him. Not YOU!

Aretha, I cared for you. I only wanted to ensure the smile I'd grown to cherish would never cease from the beauty of thy face. I hoped after time you would return to me. Yet, it seems I have brought forth the opposite of my intentions.

And I hope you suffer for what you have done, Aretha retorted by stomping on the ground with her hoof in anger. *Even in the afterlife, I will long for him.* Then her wicked laughter erupted as she threw the mane of her head up and down, followed by a harsh remark. *It seems you thought physical contact would keep the power of love from me. You see, love has many levels, but the most powerful of all is the heart. That I'm proud to say, not even a god such as you can put a stop to. The curse you placed on me may take my life, but you could not stop nor will you ever cease me from loving Alaois. An eternity of everlasting devotion will be for one. This you must live with. This is my curse I place on YOU!*

The skies once covered in baby blue with no clouds in sight, all of a sudden turned black as night. Raging seawaters and high winds erupted around her at hurricane strength. The white silk strands of her mane blew forcefully across her face.

Abruptly a bolt of lightning belted from the heavens, and struck Aretha. An electrical pulse shot through her entire body. Every cell burned, setting off tremors throughout. She tried to run, but no longer possessed the strength. A sharp pain in her chest caught her breath. Both her hands came to rest over her heart. Human hands replaced the Pegasus forelegs. Looking up at the sky, it appeared dark, even though she knew the hours of the day were still early.

The time had arrived. Neptune's curse set into motion, running its course through her until death took her.

Collapsing onto her knees, she wept; burying her face in her hands, shaking her head back and forth. She wished she could have seen Alaois one last time. One kiss goodbye would satisfy. To pass on to the afterlife with the memory of how his soft firm full lips felt on hers, a touch—just a touch. Breathing became difficult as Aretha fell onto her side and curled into a ball on the bed of sand. Vision blurry, fading with each second, she felt a splash of water smack against her. The tide rushed in toward her, the waters used in place of Neptune's hands reaching, ready to take her out to sea.

Just as darkness crept in, taking hold, it occurred to her it didn't matter the outcome of where her body drifted. Her spirit would no doubt travel to the afterlife, but would always long for the place that meant the most to her, a thirst for the Sea of Marmara where she first found love.

CHAPTER FOURTEEN

Carefully ripping away the bandages around his chest and stomach, Alaois gazed down at his healed flesh. Running his fingertips across his ribbed abs and upper torso, he grinned to see his body recovered. The bottles and bottles of his own blood and liquid from the gems did their job perfectly and he felt restored.

Getting dressed, he quickly pulled on a pair of jeans and boots then went to the back of his closet, lit by only one candle he willed to life. He removed a white button down shirt folded neatly on one of his stone shelves. He needed to look his best when he paid his last respects to his truemate who stole his heart and sacrificed hers. For if the gods cursed her to the afterlife, he would make sure he sent her there with his undying oath of love.

Making his way down the tunnel from his chambers and entering the middle gathering room, he halted to look at his men.

Stavros sat at the table, elbows resting on top of the rustic wood, face covered in his palms.

"Do not mourn for me, my friend. I am recovered as you can see," Alaois announced, walking over, if for nothing but to prove his statement intending to dispel the concerns which obviously consumed his friend.

Without turning around, Stavros spoke into his hands, which he now rubbed up and down his face with frustration. "It's not that I worry for your recovery, my lord. I know you will be heading above ground at nightfall. But I must ask…need I come with you?"

Clamping his hand on his warrior's shoulder, Alaois spoke, "Do you know out of all the men, it is you and I who have been through the most fucking shit! For I know you and you alone, are responsible for my recovery and it will never be forgotten. But, yes, my friend. You know me all too well. For this, I must do and do alone. Twilight is within minutes and I will make my leave. But I will say this…I make an oath to you now of my certain return. An oath, I have never broken." He squeezed his shoulder.

Stavros dropped his hands, smacking them upon the table. Without looking at his leader and esteemed friend, he nodded with acceptance.

When Alaois made his way down the tunnel, he heard Driscoll and the other men call out to him as they entered the room. Because of their late entrance, they caught only the back of Alaois.

His gigantic broad shouldered shadow disappeared and without a word spoken to them, he left.

"Let him go. For he will return and we all shall be gathered here and waiting; to mourn and lament alongside him for the loss of one whom he held close to his heart."

It touched him hearing Stavros' words echo down the passageway stopping the men from following and he couldn't help but crack a half smile as he headed out through the tunnel.

When the men started to head toward the tunnel, regardless of his words, Stavros stood and growled.

"I said…LET. HIM. GO! He went off to grieve and *will* be left alone. Do not make me have to show you what I mean by this."

The men backed away.

Driscoll and Braden flipped Stavros off for his outburst and headed toward their chambers.

"Shit man, we get it." Driscoll snarled.

"We know you're angry Alaois didn't take you with him, but don't take your rejection out on us," Braden added.

The others, Addison and Dagda went to the wine cellar, no doubt to appease their hunger.

As the men trickled off, Stavros stared at the now empty and quiet tunnel way. He hoped Alaois would somehow find peace in what he needed to do. He wasn't angry Alaois didn't accept his offer to join him. What disturbed him…who or what was this woman his leader risked his very life for? If she was dead, what changes would he find in Alaois when he returned? Wishing he'd known what his friend encountered and now suffered with, the best he could do was give him time…that he could do.

CHAPTER FIFTEEN

Head heavy, shoulders slumped, and with one step after the other, Alaois made his way down along the seashore. The full moon cascaded its soft beams across the crystals of sand; even the seashells sparkled. Stopping every few feet, he picked wild flowers along the edge of woods. His destination, the place he first caught Aretha's scent.

For the first time in centuries, tears swelled in his eyes as he took the long mournful walk. Halfway down the shores, the moon slowly passed behind clouds retracting its light. For a while, Alaois traveled in darkness. It matched how he felt, empty and desolate.

A few minutes passed and the lonesome moon returned. In restoring its glow, it emphasized an object across the shoreline. Panic rose as his keen sight locked in on a body being pushed up the sands by brutal tidal waves.

Long silvery strands of hair mingling with the salty pools of water. Alaois took off at the speed of light. Stopping inches away, the slenderness of the person's back faced him. He wasn't able to move, nor speak. His fingers squeezed the bouquet of fresh flowers while he bent down to turn the body over. Legs giving out, he fell to his knees. A shaky hand reached out and palmed a slender shoulder. Carefully pulling the body onto its back, Aretha's lifeless pale face stared back at him. There was no need to feel for a pulse, his senses told him she was already more than halfway to the afterlife.

Tossing the bouquet of flowers to the side, he wrapped his loving arms around her, cradling her and pulled her up into his lap, rocking her frail body back and forth. His head shot upward at the star infested sky and roared. "Arreetthhaaa!" Returning his gaze to her, he brushed wet strands of hair away from her face. He palmed the side of her cheek and leaned forward placing a kiss gently on her lips before resting his forehead against hers. More overcrowding tears pushed droplets down his despondent face. He wept harder than he had in his whole existence.

Unexpectedly, he stopped the rocking and jerked his head up. On impulse, his sharp monstrous fangs elongated from his mouth and he roared into the night. Not a second in haste, he sunk them into her neck, allowing his venom to infiltrate her body. Pulling back and licking the traces of her blood from his mouth, he ripped a gash on the inside of his arm. With the back of her head resting in his palm, Alaois placed his torn flesh, now gushing with blood over Aretha's mouth. Her lips parted as he wiggled his arm back and forth, and his blood drifted freely down her throat. So close to death, with his venom and birth born vampire blood, she would awaken a vamplin.

The last thing he'd wanted was to turn her, but a stronger dread of losing her triggered the decision. *This way, they could at least be together.* He hoped.

Dry heaving and taking huge pulls of breath, Aretha inhaled—salty sea air? How could that be? Her eyes drifted open and instantly stared at Alaois' beautiful dark eyes. But what she couldn't pull her gaze away from was the blood on the edges of his mouth, and then felt a sharp pain at the side of her neck. *Oh no.* Did he turn her? Was she now a vampire? Taking in a long lungful of air, she felt as vigorous as when she was a goddess. *How strange.* The energy and power enraptured her as it once did. Every part of her confirmed her immortal spirit had returned.

"Aretha!" Alaois gasped. He squeezed her tightly within his arms.

At the same time, Neptune's voice wailed around them in the night. "How dare you! How dare you break the spell I placed upon her!"

"Neptune," Aretha whispered.

"Let him come. He won't take you from me, again!" Alaois claimed.

"It is not wise to anger a god, blood sucker." Neptune retorted.

"You don't frighten me!"

"STOP!" Aretha yelled while getting to her feet. Alaois held onto her arm as she leaned her weight against him, her strength not fully returned. She took a few steps forward, staring up at the stars. "Tell me, how is it I'm not in the afterlife?"

"Tsk. Tsk. Tsk. Yes, I for one must admit, I did not see this coming. I should have paid closer attention to your vampire."

"What does he have to do with this?"

"Aww, my sweet. Your blood-thirsty vampire will understand when I say, liquid from our sacred gems runs through his veins and when he gave you his blood to turn you, the liquid from the ice crystals broke the curse."

"But how—why?" Aretha asked. Looking at a stunned Alaois, Aretha parted her lips to speak.

"The *gem of life* was created by my hands," Neptune continued, "Thus, whoever consumes the liquid within, will bestow its powers of healing and a bond far more powerful. When Alaois made you drink from him, your heart still beat within your chest. The liquid from the crystals broke all matters of death from you, even my curse."

"So, she isn't a vamplin?" Alaois asked, a sense of relief in his voice.

"No fiend! She will never be one of the damned such as you. Aretha is now as she once was…a goddess."

"If I am, then how is it I can see him," Aretha took Alaois' hand in hers. For she knew a goddess could never look upon the dammed.

A growl erupted from Neptune, apparently it agitated him to answer. "Your love is pure, Aretha. Fate and Zeus has blessed the two of you. For that, neither I nor the goddess Adonia who condoned the curse can dispute it. Stay with him if that is your wish. By Zeus' command, I can interfere no longer." With his words spoken, a gust of wind blew from out of nowhere. As quickly as it emerged, it was gone. Neptune's spirit returned to the heavens, never to appear again.

The instant Alaois sensed the spirit of the god was gone; he touched the side of Aretha's face and pulled her closer against him. His heart swelled at the contact. Nothing in the world from this day forth would top the love he felt for this woman. A sense of relief overcame him to know she wasn't a vamplin and would never suffer as his men did with bloodlust.

Suddenly with her face cupped in his palm, Alaois swiftly jerked her up in his arms and treaded down the beach toward the woodland. Reaching blades of soft grass, he lowered her down and captured her mouth in a kiss.

CHAPTER SIXTEEN

Alaois laid her on top of a soft patch of grass, and thanks to the gracious beams of light from the moon, she'd been able to watch him.

The sexy Vamp took a few steps backward and one by one, removed each article of clothing until he stood completely naked. His arousal jerked against his naval, his dark eyes raged with desire.

Aretha grinned and her cheeks flushed while gazing at the man she loved. A pool of wetness rushed at her core, her heart racing with a thirst of its own. Damn…how she loved this man.

One step after another, he progressed forward.

With each step taken, his six foot five majestic body and bulging erect sex had her heart rate increasing with anticipation. She day dreamed about this moment, but seeing him like this, she wanted to demand he burn all of his clothing and stay in this form forever.

Alaois knelt down by her feet and took the bottom of her gown, slowly raising it up over her head. A growl erupted from within his chest as he scanned over each part of her body. No undergarments had she ever worn. His erection poked at her core as he leaned over her.

Aretha' body temperature rose and she began to tremble. Her breath caught while she gazed up along his body and found his loving dark chocolate eyes staring intensely at her. "I love you," she said running her fingers through his hair, pulling his head forward.

"And I'm about to show you just how much I love you, woman," Alaois whispered to her ear in a husky voice, "You are…picturesque. Such beauty should not be captured by my tainted eyes."

Crooking her finger seductively for him to come even closer, if it were possible, she took control and raised her body off the ground, supporting her weight with her elbows seizing his inviting lips. Her tongue entered his welcoming mouth, locking their lips with a kiss.

Alaois gripped Aretha's waist, sliding her body further underneath him. Then, he grasped one of Aretha's legs, wrapping it behind his back. Palming the back of her neck, he pulled her body a few inches off the ground never breaking their kiss. Their tongues coiled with rapid thrusts, a covetousness of need for too long without the satisfying of desires they felt for one another.

Aretha felt Alaois spread her legs wider before a finger ran along her wet center folds and entered her steaming sex canal followed by another until three fingers penetrated her. Aretha arched her back welcoming the entry and couldn't hold back a moan from the satisfaction. "I want to feel you inside me," she groaned.

Alaois didn't disappoint. Withdrawing his fingers, he took hold of his rock hard shaft and guided it till the tip nudged at her hot sex.

Aretha screamed his name into the salty air.

With a rapid thrust, Alaois entered her all the way to the hilt.

Hell, this time they both screamed.

His shaft plunged in and out, the faster his penetrations, the wetter she became. Her coconut and citrus juices covered his cock, boosting it to life like a B12 shot. "Shit woman, I can't…"

Aretha cried. Her inner walls clenched as her orgasmic release exploded. Alaois couldn't hold back, the spasm of his climax erupted, shooting hot seed into her body.

Aretha took hold of his upper arms and squeezed. The tighter her grip became on him, the more he came inside her. Finally, Alaois pulled back. In unison, they panted, trying to gather their own strength and breath.

Side by side, Alaois' arms were wrapped around Aretha as they both stared up at the moon. The salty sea air mixed with sweet citrus and coconut to make the coupling complete and perfect.

Aretha lay quietly beside Alaois for a long while. Eventually with his eyes closed, he played with a few strands of Aretha's hair. With her finger, she traced the outline of his lips, "I hope the rest of our life together feels as good as this."

Alaois opened his eyes and tilted his head to look at her, then gently reigned kisses on her forehead, nose, and then her succulent lips. "Woman," he spoke against her lips now, "With you in my arms, I can't imagine life getting any better."

EPILOGUE

Hand in hand, Alaois guided Aretha along a long darkened tunnel. Light appeared every several feet as he willed candles to life whenever they reached them. When he pushed open a heavy metal door, he could see all the men were gathered as usual. He could hear conversations being discussed before entering. Yet, the second he pushed open the door with Aretha at his side, silence fell across the room.

Multiple throats cleared in the air, all gazes were glued on his woman.

Aretha's hand tightened within his grasp as she moved closer against him.

Alaois squeezed back, to reassure her. "Men, this is Aretha, my truemate. She is here to join us," he spoke proudly.

None of the men uttered a word. Their glances remained fixated on Aretha.

At their stunned expressions and mute reactions, Alaois burst into laughter and headed toward an entrance, leading to his personal chambers. Still hand in hand, he and Aretha walked across the quiet room, all eyes no doubt following their every step.

When they reached the hallway, an odd thudding sound came from behind them.

Alaois and Aretha spun around to find all five men upon bended knee. Their heads tilted downward, and lowered in absolute reverence.

Alaois felt stunned by this homage, by such proud warriors, but what moved him the most was each of them held one hand over their heart while their other palm pressed flat down against the cool stone floor. Aretha wouldn't know the high regard of respect they presented, but Alaois did.

The heart meant love and the ground, signified home. They accepted and welcomed her as their own.

"They like you. In all ways, they welcome you to the clan and will serve you as they do me. This is a very high honor and you will never find a greater group of men to ensure your safety."

Alaois didn't expect Aretha to do anything, yet surprisingly, she unlocked their hands and advanced toward his men. No fear in her actions at all.

His supposedly nonexistent soul vibrated with joy watching his truemate approach the lethal vamplin warriors.

She stopped in front of them, their positions unmoving as they flanked one another in a straight line. One by one, Aretha gently touched the tops of their shoulders with the tips of her fingers as she moved along the line of them. A glow suddenly emitted from where her fingers touched them. "We will forever be bonded you and I," she spoke kindly to all of them.

The men tilted their heads upward, a look of admiration shown on each of their faces.

"I know now I have found the family I was meant to have. No matter where we are, I will always be able to find you. In your station to protect me and…" Aretha glanced over her shoulder and her smile grew wider when she stared at Alaois, "…the love of my whole existence. You should know with this bond, if any harm comes to you, I will find you and aid you in your time of need. This is the gift I give to each of you." Quietly, she turned around and moved back to Alaois' side.

He took her hand in his and with the other, cupped the side of her face with a gentle pride at the gift she'd given his men. In a sudden hasty movement, he then scooped her up in his arms and carried swiftly her down the hallway. Then, he couldn't help but laugh when he heard Braden sarcastically utter, "I have a feeling, this time…We better make sure *not* to disturb him."

ABOUT THE AUTHOR

Scarlet Hunter by day, works full time as a Director for a TPA (Third Party Administrator) company for Section 125 benefit plans. Residing in the outskirts of Memphis, Tennessee, when not working at her full-time job, she is found typing away on her laptop. Scarlet released her first self-publication in February 2013 with Curator's Curse, Book One of Legends of the Immortal Bloods Series. As an avid reader, Scarlet's love of science-fiction/paranormal romances inspired her to pursue her dream of writing. You can visit her at www.scarlethunter.com to find all the great stuff in the works.

OTHER BOOKS

BY

SCARLET HUNTER

Dust of Darkness, Book One, The Reign of Darkness
Curator's Curse, Book One
Legends of the Immortal Bloods

Coming in 2014

-Snowline's Visitor, Book One,
Arise of the Guardians
-Heaven's Sacrifice
-Burning Salvation

Coming in 2015

Mid-Night Mountain, Book Two,
Arise of the Guardians

Demon's Light, Book Two,
The Reign of Darkness